SUNSHINE STABLES

Jess was aware of being thrown backwards and forwards, as Bandit first bucked with such ferocity that his nose almost touched the sand, then humped his back and leapt upwards, throwing Jess between his ears and back again. She was falling, and she couldn't stop herself...

SUNSHINE
STABLES

Have you read?

POPPY *and the* PERFECT PONY
SOPHIE *and the* SPOOKY PONY
GRACIE *and the* GRUMPY PONY

Coming soon:

AMINA *and the* AMAZING PONY
WILLOW *and the* WHIZZY PONY

SUNSHINE STABLES

JESS and the
JUMPY PONY

OLIVIA TUFFIN

ILLUSTRATED BY
JO GOODBERRY

nosy crow

FOR ISLA

First published in the UK in 2022 by Nosy Crow Ltd
The Crow's Nest, 14 Baden Place, Crosby Row
London, SE1 1YW, UK

Nosy Crow and associated logos are trademarks and/or registered
trademarks of Nosy Crow Ltd

Text copyright © Olivia Tuffin, 2022
Illustrations copyright © Jo Goodberry, 2022

978 1 78800 957 7

A CIP catalogue record for this book will be available from the British Library.

Printed and bound in the UK by Clays Ltd, Elcograf S.p.A.

Papers used by Nosy Crow are made from wood grown in
sustainable forests.

1 3 5 7 9 10 8 6 4 2

MIX
Paper from
responsible sources
FSC® C018072

www.nosycrow.com

CHAPTER 1

Jess felt a rush of disappointment as she clutched Merlin's lead rope tighter. Merlin was a beautiful grey Connemara pony, and Jess had been partnered with him for her week at Sunshine Stables Pony Camp. Merlin shifted his weight and Jess ran her hand over his neck.

"Is he hurt?" she asked nervously as Zoe, the groom, straightened up after inspecting Merlin's foot. Zoe nodded. The kind grey pony stood quietly, nuzzling against Jess's hand, ears pricked forwards.

Jess had known something was wrong the minute she had gone to get Merlin in from the

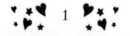

field. They had enjoyed a brilliant cross-country lesson that morning. Merlin had been flying over everything – the brush, the tyres and even the tricky drop fence. Merlin was a talented pony and Jess knew it was a real honour to ride him.

Lainey, who owned the riding school where the camps were held, kept all sorts of ponies, mostly safe schoolmasters or mistresses. From dear Henry, a trustworthy dark bay, to Gorse, a cheeky Exmoor. But Lainey also had a couple of ponies suitable for more experienced riders. There was Misty, another grey, and Merlin, standing about fourteen hands. He was a brilliant jumper, and had won loads of events.

"He's not a novice ride," Lainey had explained. "But he's willing and fun. You'll have an amazing time!"

And Jess *had* had an amazing time so far. With lessons, and hacking, and looking after a pony for a whole week as if it was your own, Sunshine Stables Pony Camp was every pony-mad child's dream!

Zoe's voice cut through her thoughts.

"It's a bruised sole, I'd bet," the groom said in a matter-of-fact voice. "He was fine when you turned him out. I expect he's trodden on a stone. I'll get Angie, our farrier, to have a look."

Zoe gave Merlin a pat, and then seemed to

notice Jess's downcast expression.

"There, there," Zoe said in a kind, but firm voice. "These things happen. Just horses, I'm afraid!" She gave a wry smile.

She's probably dealt with a hundred lame horses over time, Jess thought. She *knew* it was no one's fault, but it didn't make it any better. And Zoe didn't know how much was at stake. Jess had been so wrapped up in caring for Merlin that it had been easy to keep the promise she'd made her parents...

"Pop him back into his stable, and give him some more shavings to make his bed extra comfortable," Zoe continued.

Feeling miserable, Jess clucked for Merlin to follow her. Merlin did so obediently, walking just a little more carefully on his sore foot. It could have been easy to miss, Jess thought. But she was really good at noticing things. Asia, her big cousin, often praised Jess for her attention to detail.

Asia was a vet. She worked in a surgery nearby and Jess spent every minute she could there. She loved helping out, making beds for the dogs who had to stay in, playing with kittens, and best of all, going out to help Asia look at horses. Sometimes she'd even get to hold their lead ropes as Asia examined legs or stitched up wounds. When she was with Asia and the animals, she was at her happiest.

But it hadn't been easy recently. She was getting into loads of bother at school, although she didn't mean to. Wherever there was some sort of animal-related trouble, Jess found herself in the middle of it! Like the time she'd found some older children in the playground teasing a pigeon with a damaged wing. The poor bird hadn't been able to fly properly and the children had been swooping in and scaring it. Jess had seen red and got between the horrid group and the bird. She hadn't *meant* to push the biggest of the boys, it had just sort of happened, but as a result she and the gang had been hauled into the headteacher's office.

"A pigeon?" The headteacher had peered at Jess over his glasses.

Jess had nodded, but had felt the swell of rage again. "It was hurt, and they were chasing it!" she'd cried as the gang shuffled their feet and avoided each other's gaze. There was no way to prove it. Jess had got away with yet another detention, but it had only made her more determined. If an animal was in danger, she would do anything to help!

But that detention had been the final straw for Jess's parents. Jess had known she was in trouble the minute she'd walked back into the house swinging her book bag. Her mum had been standing against the kitchen counter, her lips tight.

"Mr Peters phoned earlier," she'd said, referring to Jess's headteacher. "Jessika, I'm not happy."

Uh-oh, her mum had used her full name, she was in big trouble. But Jess also knew her mum usually tried to see her side. Her mum loved animals too. It ran in their family.

"Sorry, Mum," she'd mumbled. "It was…"

"A pigeon," her mum had sighed, her face softening. "I know. Mr Peters explained. Jess, you know how proud I am of your passion for animals. But…" Jess had winced at the change of tone as her mum continued, "It's no good if you get into trouble, or don't concentrate on your schoolwork. Mr Peters said you didn't make any effort in your maths test."

"I did!" Jess had protested, but she knew she hadn't, not really. She'd spent most of the time staring out of the window at a lady walking a gorgeous retriever around the edge of the playing field.

Her mum had then given her *that* look. "I've been chatting to your dad," she'd said, and Jess had inwardly groaned. She loved her dad, who lived nearby, but he was even hotter on schoolwork than her mum. Her parents got on pretty well despite their divorce, but Jess knew if her mum and her dad had joined forces, things were serious.

"Mr Peters told me about a homework club they have on Monday nights," her mum had continued. "I think it would be a good idea. Then we thought you could join netball on Wednesdays. Mr Peters said you're really good, and don't you think it would be nice to see the girls in your class outside the school day?"

Jess had known what her mum was implying. She never went shopping in town or hung out at the rec. She liked her classmates well enough, but there was no one she was particularly close to. She often talked about what she did at Asia's, but the last time she'd come into school totally enthused about something she'd watched, her friends had been completely grossed out.

"Ewwwwww!" Mollie, one of her classmates had visibly paled as Jess described the blood. "That's disgusting! Ew, don't tell me any more – I'll throw up."

So Jess hadn't. No one really understood anyway. And shopping and hanging out at the rec felt like a waste of time when there were animals to look after.

"So Mondays, and Wednesdays," her mum had said. "From September. I don't think we've got a choice."

Mondays and Wednesdays, Jess had thought in horror. Those were the days Asia had asked her to help with the new puppy classes, starting in the autumn. They were her first big responsibility. She'd felt her stomach drop.

"No, Mum," she'd said. "I can't. I'd miss the puppy classes – the ones I told you about. I promise, I promise I'll try harder at school."

But Jess knew her mum was considering it, and as a result of the detention, Jess had been banned from Asia's surgery for a week. That had been the worst bit. But then her mum had seen an advert for pony camp in the paper.

"I think you'd love this," she'd said one

evening, and Jess had nodded, a smile creeping across her face.

"That would be amazing, Mum. Thank you."

Jess had learnt to ride as a young child. Her mum had taken her to visit a horsey friend one summer when they'd been on a camping holiday. Jess had learnt to canter and jump, her bravery and natural talent shining through. She loved all animals, but horses were her passion. A week at pony camp, looking after a pony as if it was her very own, would be everything she'd dreamt of! But there was more too.

"Your dad and I agree the puppy classes *are* a great opportunity for you. If you can stay out of trouble, get a bit of work done in the holidays and show us how committed you are to school then we'll let you do the classes with Asia. But any trouble," she'd added sternly, "and that's it. I'll be signing you straight up for homework and netball club." She'd then smiled. "But you can't exactly get into bother spending a while with the horses, can you?"

And Jess had shaken her head vigorously. This was her chance!

"No way," she'd grinned. "Ponies, and nothing else. No trouble. I *promise!*"

CHAPTER 2

A short while later, Angie the farrier confirmed Zoe's thoughts.

"Nothing more than a slight bruise," Angie said cheerfully, rolling down the sleeves of her boiler suit. She had curly red hair fastened in place with a biro. "A few days off and he should be as right as rain. Bad luck for you though," she added, seeming to notice Jess's expression. "I'm sure Lainey will find another pony for you to ride."

"Of course," Lainey, who had just joined them, smiled. "Jess is a lovely rider so I'm confident she'll bring out the best in any pony. Though I might have to swap a little bit with the others, or perhaps arrange a pony share."

Jess nodded, but now felt even worse. She knew she was lucky to be taking part in camp – Lainey had a long waiting list – and she knew the more ponies she got to ride, the more experienced she'd be. But she *had* enjoyed riding Merlin, and now everything was going to change. She felt her tummy twist anxiously. What if she argued with one of the other camp members over pony sharing, or was somehow blamed for Merlin's injury? She'd done so well to stay out of any trouble so far.

"This definitely proves I need to buy another school pony though," Lainey continued in a thoughtful voice. "It's just a matter of finding one."

"I'll ask around," Angie said. "You could put up an advert in Mandy's saddlery, and the vets' receptions."

"Did you know Jess's cousin is a vet?" Lainey said. "Asia Kowalski – she works at the Greengage Practice."

Angie smiled at Jess. "How nice!" she said. "Is that what you want to do, too? Something with animals?"

Jess nodded.

"I want to be a vet like Asia," she explained. "I've known since I was little."

And Jess thought back to the teddy bears with bandaged paws: she'd spend hours wrapping real-life vet wrap around her toys' legs, and giving them pretend medicine with a plastic syringe. Working in a real-life vet's clinic had been amazing, and even better when Asia had asked her to help with the puppy classes.

Jess was nearly halfway through camp now, and she knew Lainey would have only good things to say so far! She just had to keep it up. Her parents' words echoed in her mind: Stay out of trouble. And it had been easy, when she had so much to do at camp with caring for Merlin. Only she no longer had a pony to ride. So what would happen now?

Once Merlin was settled in his stable, Jess closed the door, trying to find the positives. Lainey had said she could ride Sorrel that afternoon, and Zebedee the next morning. Sorrel was a lovely mare, but she was definitely a pony for a real novice, as was fluffy Zebedee. It would still be fun though, Jess told herself firmly.

"I'm sorry about Merlin!" A cheerful voice Jess

recognised as belonging to Sophie, one of her friends, carried over the yard. Sophie was good fun and rode the cheeky Exmoor, Gorse. Skipping over, Sophie put her arm through Jess's. "Oh look, there's Emily," she continued. "Wonder what she's got to moan about now!"

Jess looked up, watching Emily cross the yard. Emily was Lainey's daughter and had a twin brother called Jack. But whereas Jack was always cheerful, Emily was the total opposite. Jess knew that Emily hated strangers looking after the horses, which Jess could sort of understand, but Lainey was always supervising them, and all the ponies were beautifully cared for.

But for once Emily didn't have anything to criticise the girls for. Instead she totally ignored Jess and Sophie and made her way over to where Lainey was helping Gracie, another camp member, put together a bridle.

"Mum," Emily said. "Remember Rhiannon and her pony are coming."

"Oh!" Lainey said. "I'd totally forgotten that was this morning. Goodness, I'd better get the stable ready. Sorry, Gracie, I'll have to come back to this later."

Feeling curious, Jess stepped closer.

"Have you got a new pony arriving?" she said, a bubble of excitement starting to grow. Perhaps Lainey had already found one!

"Well," Lainey said. "Yes and no. I'm not sure how I got roped into it, but one of Emily's schoolfriends has a pony, and her mum is dropping him off here whilst they go on holiday. The pony is for sale, and they are paying me to have him here so people can come and look at him. They said something about him not getting on with their other pony." Lainey looked at her daughter. "What's his name again? I've been so busy."

"Bandit," muttered Emily, not looking at Jess.

"That's it," Lainey said. "Bandit. Right, I'd better get his stable ready."

Lainey looked hot and flustered, Jess thought. She was used to helping out so stepped forwards.

"Do you want me to do it?" she asked and Lainey nodded, looking relieved.

"That would be amazing, Jess, thank you," she said. "I was going to put him in the old foaling box, so he's out of the way of the main yard. It's lovely and big."

Jess smiled. "Of course," she said. "Do you want to help me, Sophie?" Sophie was good fun and the two girls could chat away as they carried out the task. Jess wanted to make Bandit's stable as nice as possible, in case he was unsettled. But mostly she was glad of the distraction. The new pony might take her mind off her worries, and she was already intrigued by the situation. Perhaps he was being bullied by the other pony, and it had been a really hard decision for his owners to take him to a different yard. She hoped they weren't feeling too upset.

CHAPTER 3

But a short while later, Jess's opinion changed. Jess and Sophie had just made up a lovely bed of shavings and tied up a hay net. A silver horse-box pulled into the yard and a girl wearing white shorts and heart-shaped sunglasses jumped out, followed by a glossy-looking mum. It had to be Rhiannon.

Emily crossed over the cobbles to meet Rhiannon, who hugged her.

"Hey, Em," Rhiannon said loudly. "How's it going?"

"Oh, great, I just—" Emily replied, but before

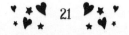

she could say any more, Rhiannon interrupted, flicking her hair back.

"Really *sucks* you can't come to Spain with us," she said, sounding anything but sorry. "You *know* I wanted to ask you, but I thought since you're always busy at the stables I'd ask Lily." She pushed her sunglasses up and gave a smile, which looked totally fake, Jess thought. "And Lily's into all the discos and the waterpark and getting dressed up and stuff, and you don't really like that kind of thing, do you? Remember the disco last term? You wore your *riding boots*."

"I thought they looked nice…"

Emily said, sounding a little doubtful. "And I suppose I don't really like discos. I like waterparks though—"

Rhiannon gave a tinkly giggle.

"Riding boots!" she repeated, interrupting Emily again. "I was sooooo embarrassed. What would you wear in Spain? Your jodhs? A body protector and crash hat?" She fell about laughing at her own joke.

Emily looked down at the ground, and Rhiannon hugged her again.

"Aw, you know I'm only joking, don't you?" she said. "You're still one of my *best* friends. Remember? St Mary's Primary pals for ever!"

Emily smiled, but looked a bit unsure.

"Of course," she said quietly.

Rhiannon was queen bee, Jess decided. She reminded her of the mean girl in her class, who'd laughed when Jess read out her poem in English, the one she'd written about the pigeon she'd tried to protect. She didn't like Rhiannon one bit. Despite how grumpy Emily could be, she found herself feeling sorry for her, and felt like giving Rhiannon a piece of her mind. But remembering her promise to her parents, she kept her mouth shut, and didn't say a word.

Lainey had joined the girls and Rhiannon's mum now.

"Hi," Lainey greeted Rhiannon's mum in a friendly voice. "Shall we get Bandit settled in? You can stay as long as you like to make sure he's OK. I know this must be really hard."

But Rhiannon's mum was already pulling the ramp of the horse-box down, and leading the most beautiful grey pony out.

"He'll be all right," she said, handing the lead rein to Lainey. "Our plane leaves this afternoon and I've still got some packing to do, and a hair

appointment, so we'd better get on actually."

"OK," Lainey said, sounding surprised. "I know we chatted on the phone, but is there anything else I need to know? Anything I need to mention to potential buyers?"

"No," Rhiannon's mum said breezily. "He just wasn't getting on with our new pony, so it was tricky. Rhiannon needs to concentrate on the Horse of the Year Show qualifier classes, not worry about Bandit. I thought it would be easier for you to sell him here, so we can go back to our other pony after our holiday without all the hassle. You know how it is."

"Right," Lainey said, frowning a little, as though she didn't know how it was at all. "Well, I've got Zoe, and plenty of help from the kids, so I'm sure we'll be fine."

She gave Bandit a pat.

"Is he OK inside at night, and outside plenty

during the day?" she then asked. "That's our normal routine."

"Oh, he's mostly in his stable," Rhiannon's mum said. "It's just easier that way, keeping him clean for shows."

"Right," Lainey said. "OK."

Jess glanced up at the paddocks above the yard. One of the things she loved most about it here was the fields full of happy, relaxed ponies, who all got plenty of turn-out between lessons to roll and gallop and get muddy. She didn't like the thought of Bandit in his stable all the time, especially on such a lovely sunny day as today.

Rhiannon's mum was in a hurry to leave, which was understandable, Jess supposed, given that their holiday flight was so soon. But as the horse-box left the yard, it suddenly struck Jess that Rhiannon hadn't patted Bandit once. She hadn't even said goodbye to him!

"Thanks, Jess," Lainey said as the lorry disappeared from sight. "Are you OK to put him in his stable? Zoe's about, but I need to get the school ponies ready."

Jess nodded. She didn't mind one bit. She liked new challenges, and she was used to settling animals. And Bandit seemed so calm and sweet. Lainey was still holding the lead rope and the grey pony was resting a leg, seemingly unbothered about the change in surroundings.

"Of course," she said, taking the rope. "Come on, boy."

Bandit walked obediently next to her as Sophie trotted alongside, chatting away. Jess had a minute to really appreciate Bandit's looks. He was an iron grey with a silky mane and tail. His eyes were large and kind and his neck had an elegant arch. He was beautiful, a little like an old-fashioned rocking horse, Jess thought.

"There you go," Jess said, giving him a pat as she slipped off his headcollar in the stable. Bandit watched everything with interest, giving Dolly, a lovely chestnut next door, a little whicker of greeting.

"He seems really friendly," Sophie remarked. "But Rhiannon's mum said he didn't get on with their other pony, didn't she?"

Jess thought about this.

"Maybe it was just that one pony," she said. "Or maybe it was *Bandit* who was being bullied?"

She wondered if she had Rhiannon all wrong. Perhaps it had been really hard for her to move Bandit, but she'd done so for his sake. But Jess couldn't forget the way the other girl had barely glanced at the pony! Something didn't add up. She just wasn't sure what…

When Sophie went to get Gorse, Jess stayed a few extra minutes with Bandit. Not only was he beautiful, she decided, but he seemed so kind and had a really sweet way of snuffling his muzzle into the crook of her arm. Giggling as his whiskers tickled her, Jess gave him a hug.

"I think you'd be really easy to fall in love with," she said, finally tearing herself away. She had to go and get Sorrel ready, but she was savouring her time with the beautiful grey pony.

And a short while later, trotting around the arena on Sorrel, Jess had a sudden thought. Lainey was looking for another pony to join the Sunshine Stables team. And Jess wondered if the answer was already in the old foaling box! She'd only known Bandit a short time, but there was something about him. Something really special.

CHAPTER 4

Jess picked her moment carefully. She'd given Sorrel a good groom after their lesson, and then turned her out into the field. She'd given Merlin a groom too, just in case he was feeling left out. As she walked back to the feed room, she saw Lainey writing up the rota on the whiteboard.

"Um," Jess said, not knowing how to start. She didn't want Lainey to think she was being cheeky. "I was just wondering about Bandit. Do you think he'd be suitable for the riding school?"

But to Jess's relief, Lainey gave her a big smile.

"Do you know," she said. "I was thinking the

same. But Bandit's done lots of showjumping, so I worried he might find riding-school life boring, and our yard is a bit scruffy compared to where he's come from."

Jess looked around, at the chickens scratching around the cobbles, and the brightly painted stable doors, and the old trough full of wildflowers.

"I think it's perfect here," she said.

"Thanks, Jess." Lainey smiled, before continuing, "However, the standard of riding amongst you kids has improved so much, and I think a pony like him might be really useful, especially with all the fun things I have planned."

Jess gave a little squeak of excitement. She knew there was no guarantee Lainey would actually buy Bandit, but this was something! And Lainey was about to make Jess's day even better.

"If we do try him out," Lainey continued. "What do you say to riding him?"

JESS and the JUMPY PONY

There was no way Jess would say no!

"Yes!" she said quick as a flash, before Lainey could change her mind. "Yes please! I'd love to!"

Then she turned, aware someone had joined them. Emily was standing there, arms folded.

"Hi, sweetheart," Lainey smiled. "How was Fable on her walk?"

Fable was Emily's pony, a sweet elderly grey who Lainey had bottle-fed as a foal when Fable's mother died shortly after the birth. Fable was very precious to Lainey and her children, particularly Emily. Jess thought about Rhiannon and the fact she hadn't patted Bandit, and the way Emily doted on Fable. She couldn't understand why Rhiannon and Emily were best friends. From the little bit she'd seen, they weren't at all alike..

"She was good, quite cheeky," Emily said, the hint of a grin appearing. It was the happiest Jess had ever seen her!

"I was just talking to Jess," Lainey said. "And we've agreed that since Bandit is already here, *and* for sale, we would try him out! You know how I was talking to Dad about a new pony the other night? He's the perfect size and seems lovely to handle too."

But Emily looked up sharply. Jess saw a strange expression flash across her face, but she wasn't sure what it was. Worry? It was so hard to tell with Emily.

Lainey didn't seem to notice.

"Don't you think that's a good idea?" she said. "Rhiannon would be pleased too, if he goes to a home she knows. She can visit him when she comes round. It seems the perfect solution."

But Emily's eyes seemed to

dart around.

"I don't know," she muttered. "I'm not sure how suitable he is."

"Well, I'll talk to Rhiannon's mum," Lainey said. "I know they wanted him to go to a competition home, a posh yard like theirs, but I think it would be worth trying him out."

Just then, there was a shout from across the yard.

"Lainey!" Zoe, the groom called. "The hay man's here."

"Coming!" Lainey called back. "The monthly hay delivery has arrived," she explained to Jess. "I'll need you kids to give me a hand later."

"Sure," Jess said.

When Lainey had gone to greet the driver of the small tractor and trailer that was waiting in the gateway, Jess turned to Emily. She wanted to find out a bit more about the gorgeous grey pony.

"Do you go to all the same shows as Bandit?" Jess asked. She knew that sometimes Lainey took Jack and Emily to local events with the more experienced ponies like Merlin and Misty.

Emily folded her arms.

"Not really," she said. "Rhiannon took him out

showjumping a bit, but then just stopped. She said he couldn't really jump the high jumps like she wanted, but…" She seemed to want to say something else but stopped herself.

"But what?" Jess said. She'd never minded being upfront about asking questions.

"It's none of your business!" Emily said crossly. "Rhiannon's my best friend and that's what she told me!"

And with that Emily strode off, leaving Jess blinking with surprise. Did Emily know something else about Bandit? What was the real reason Rhiannon had stopped taking the little grey pony to shows?

CHAPTER 5

Jess tried to forget Emily's puzzling comment as she tacked Bandit up later, marvelling at the beautifully cut saddle of the softest leather and the gold embroidered saddle cloth with matching brushing boots. Rhiannon didn't seem to care much for Bandit but he sure had some gorgeous tack! Jess felt a jolt of excitement in her tummy. From feeling so down over Merlin, to the thrill of trying out a beautiful pony like Bandit – camp was really looking up!

"Wow!" Amina, who rode little Nutmeg, peered over the door.

"Jess, he's gorgeous!" Poppy, another of Jess's friends, had joined Amina and was also looking at Bandit in admiration. "Fingers crossed he's the one for Sunshine Stables!"

"I hope so," Jess said, nerves now mixing with her excitement. Not that she was worried about riding a new pony, but more that in such a short space of time she had fallen head over heels for Bandit, and longed for Lainey to buy him. It was like it was meant to be!

Tightening the girth, she gave a start as Bandit put his ears back for the first time since his arrival, flinging his head up and down.

"I'm sorry!" Jess stroked his neck. "Did I do it up too quickly?" She knew some ponies could be sensitive about being girthed, and she vowed to take more care next time. Bandit snuffled at her hands, ears forward again, as if forgiving her. Leading him out, Jess swung lightly into the saddle, giving Bandit a pat as they headed towards the outdoor arena.

"Lovely," Lainey said with a smile as Bandit walked eagerly through the gate, his ears pricked. "You look really good on him, Jess." And Jess felt her heart swell with pride.

She walked Bandit round on both reins, before asking him to trot on. He was gorgeous, she thought. So responsive but not silly, forward going without Jess having to pull him back. His trot was springy and light and his canter was like that of a rocking horse, striking off on the right leg each time. He was engaged and obedient and completed the most perfect figures of eight and serpentines as Jess put him through his paces. She barely had to use her legs at all, he reacted so readily to her voice. She was smiling so much, her cheeks were starting to hurt. She loved him!

"Brilliant!" Lainey sounded delighted, Jess thought happily. "I think he could be right. Don't you?" She laughed as Jess nodded her head enthusiastically.

"Definitely!" Jess called back.

"I'll put up a little jump," Lainey then said, arranging the poles into an inviting cross-pole and spread combination. Jess circled Bandit in canter and aimed him towards the first jump, anticipating his next move to be soaring over the poles as gracefully as a bird. He did exactly

that, and she was delighted as the pink and white poles disappeared under his neat hooves. Then Jess turned Bandit towards the small spread. She barely had to touch him with her heels. Once again, he sailed over it, landing perfectly, his ears pricked.

"Lovely!" Lainey was over the moon. "I'll put them up a bit. Just keep your leg on now, as you'll need to ride forward."

Jess grinned. Bandit was the most amazing pony she'd ever ridden! Her heart lifted as she aimed once again for the cross-pole, pressing her heels to his sides.

It all happened so fast.

Jess was aware of being thrown backwards and forwards, as Bandit first bucked with such ferocity that his nose almost touched the sand, then humped his back and leapt upwards, throwing Jess between his ears and back again. She was falling, and she couldn't stop herself. The ground rushed up to meet her as she sprawled on the sand, feeling the breath knocked hard from her body as she did so.

Immediately, she knew it was a bad fall. Gingerly she stretched her arms and legs. Nothing seemed broken, but she really hurt! And Bandit, where was he? Lifting her head, Jess saw the grey pony careering around as Zoe ran to catch him and Lainey rushed to Jess. He looked so panicked, Jess thought. She had to get to him. Clambering up, she felt Lainey's hands on her shoulders, forcing her to stay where she was.

"Hang on," Lainey said gently, peering at Jess. "Not so fast. We need to check you're OK."

"I'm fine," Jess muttered, reaching up to her face as she felt a warm trickle coming down her chin. Her lip was bleeding, she realised. She must have bitten it as she landed. No wonder Lainey looked so worried.

"Goodness, Jess," Lainey said anxiously. "That was a really nasty fall. No one could have sat that buck."

"I really *am* OK," Jess said, wiping her chin. Despite feeling horribly winded, she was only worried about Bandit. Glancing over, she saw Zoe had got hold of him. "I must get back on."

"No, absolutely not," Lainey said firmly, helping Jess to her feet now she seemed confident she hadn't broken anything. "Let's get that lip sorted out and Zoe can untack Bandit."

"But it's my fault!" Jess protested. "I probably put him on the wrong stride, or perhaps I accidentally caught him in the mouth…"

But Lainey was shaking her head.

"No," she repeated. "You rode him beautifully – you didn't do a thing wrong. He just exploded out of nowhere. I'm afraid that answers our question as to his suitability as a riding-school pony. That was just dangerous."

Jess's heart sank. Her throat felt all lumpy and she couldn't help but believe she'd totally messed up! But there was something else too. Bandit had acted in a way that was so out of character – like a different pony to the one she'd got to know since his arrival – that there *had* to be a reason for it. Zoe led him away back to the yard as Lainey helped a hobbling Jess back to the house. Jess saw Bandit turn his head to her, as if searching for her with his dark eyes. *Like he's asking me for help,* Jess thought with a jolt. What did he want her to understand?

A bit later, Jess sat in the cool of Lainey's kitchen with a lemonade. Amina and Poppy had joined her for support. The cut on Jess's lip had turned out to be small, the blood making it look more dramatic than it was and she felt less wobbly now. Her only concern was Bandit, but Lainey was firm.

"I'm sorry, Jess," Lainey said, refilling their glasses, "but I can't risk taking on a pony like that."

"But there must have been a

reason," Jess said miserably as Amina gave her arm a squeeze.

Lainey looked thoughtful.

"Yes, there probably is, but he *could* just be a difficult pony. Rhiannon had stopped taking him to shows, and I don't know why," she said. "When I try out a pony for the stables, they have to be perfect from the word go. I can't take on a pony with any issues."

Jess nodded. She knew Lainey was right. But she also *knew* it hadn't been Bandit's fault!

"I'm really sorry," Poppy said quietly as Lainey tidied things away. "I know how much you liked him."

And Jess could only blink away tears. She'd already lost Merlin for the week, and now she was going to lose Bandit too. She'd found her perfect pony, and now he would be taken away!

CHAPTER 6

Jess had managed to sneak into Bandit's stable to check he was OK. There *had* to be something behind his behaviour – she just knew it. Something about jumping bigger, and her nudging him on, had caused that extreme reaction.

As she put her arms around his strong grey neck, Jess's mind was racing, wondering what she could do.

But her day was about to get even worse. Hearing footsteps outside, Jess looked up as Bandit pricked his ears in welcome. It was Lainey, and she was leaning against the door.

"I've just been talking to Rhiannon's mum – I finally managed to get through to her mobile in Spain," she said gently. "She was adamant Bandit hadn't done anything like that before, and told me he did need an experienced showjumping home. She was … er, quite blunt."

Jess hugged Bandit tighter.

"I think there's something wrong with him!" she said. "He's in pain, or uncomfortable. He can't be sold until they find out what the problem is!"

Lainey's face clouded over, and it looked as though she wanted to say something. There was a pause.

"The trouble is," Lainey began, "Bandit's not mine. I agreed he could come here whilst his owners went away – the money is going to be very useful for feeding the ponies over winter – but I'm afraid it's not up to me what happens to him. I wish…" She stopped herself, and shook her head. "I'm sorry to tell you, Jess, but Rhiannon's mum has arranged for someone to come and try him this afternoon. An experienced showjumper!"

"We have to do something!"

Jess was sitting on the floor of the camp barn, her friends around her. Their *Pony*-magazine quiz had been abandoned as Jess burst back in, her face tear streaked. Amina and Poppy had filled the others in on what Lainey had said, but Jess had now told her friends the worst bit of all, the fact that someone was coming to try him out.

"There must be something we can do," she continued with a sniff. "He can't be sold. Not the

way he is!"

"What *could* we do though?" Willow said. Willow was kind, but she could be straight-talking. "I mean, if Lainey says so, that's that, isn't it? He's not actually hers."

Jess remembered Lainey's expression, when Jess had told her she thought Bandit might be in pain. She *knew* Lainey agreed with her. But Willow was right. She sighed miserably.

"Or," Gracie said with a smile, and everyone

turned to look at her, "we could work together, try and put the buyers off…"

A slow smile of understanding crept across Sophie's face.

"Gracie, I get it!" she said. "You're an actress, aren't you? You mean we could all say things, act a bit, and scare them away?"

Gracie nodded, looking at Jess.

"Exactly that!" she said. "What do you think?"

Jess paused. She knew she was supposed to stay out of trouble, and it wouldn't do to interfere with the sale. But if they didn't actually say anything *directly* to the buyers, no one could prove anything, could they? She turned to Gracie. It was a big risk, they would have to be subtle, but perhaps they could pull it off!

"I think you're a genius," she said. "Let's do it!"

"OK now, are you ready?"

JESS and the JUMPY PONY

Jess wished they had some walkie-talkies! It was a little later, and the friends were ready to put their plan into action. She and Gracie had organised where everyone would stand, as if they were just doing their normal pony chores, ready for the potential buyers to come into the yard.

Sophie and Amina were going to sweep the path along to Bandit's stable, and Willow and Poppy were cleaning their tack on the wooden bar in the middle of the yard. Gracie, the best actress, was going to hover near the big gates, whereas Jess, who had already sorted Merlin's stable, just wanted to be near Bandit. From across the yard, Gracie gave her a thumbs up.

As a car pulled slowly up to the gates, Jess watched as Lainey hurried over. It was now or never!

A pleasant-looking woman in jeans hopped out, followed by a girl about Jess's age. She clutched

her hat and gazed around, an excited look on her face. She had lovely riding clothes on and there was a Horse of the Year Show sticker on the back windscreen. Jess felt a stab of envy. She wished she was looking for her own pony, but she knew she was really lucky to ride at Sunshine Stables, and also to help Asia on her horse visits. She couldn't let that stop, she thought. She had to stay out of trouble. She *had* to be extra careful here…

But as the woman and her daughter walked alongside Lainey, Jess moved a little closer, to see if she could work out what was being said.

"We've spoken to the owner," the woman was telling Lainey. "And she said Bandit was perfect for Ava." The woman gestured to her daughter. "We have a lovely home waiting."

Jess imagined Ava jumping huge fences, and the neat stables in her back garden, and her travelling to big shows all over the country.

"I'll get his tack," Lainey said. She looked anxious, Jess thought. "Ava, are you happy to ride him today?"

"Of course!" Ava grinned. "I'm so excited!"

Lainey looked as though she was stalling for time.

"I have a better idea, perhaps you could just meet him today, and ride him when his owners are back," she said. "What about that?"

"No," Ava said. "I want to ride him today."

"And did his owners tell you everything you need to know? Did they say he had any vices?" Lainey said with a frown.

Ava's mum looked a little irritated now.

"No, and we'll ride him today, as Ava said," she said pleasantly, but there was an edge to her voice. "I've had a long telephone conversation with his owner and they think we'd be perfect for him. They said he wasn't right for your riding school, that he needed a private home. We have the best trainer in the whole of the South of England ready to teach Ava and our yard is top class. So if you don't mind, this is between us, and his *owners.*"

As Lainey headed towards the tack room, Jess nodded at Gracie, who was pretending to pull up weeds from between the cobbles. Nodding back, Gracie straightened up and then with an exaggerated wince and groan started to hobble over the yard. Taking her cue, Sophie ran over.

"Gracie!" Sophie cried, loud enough so Ava and her mum looked over. "Are you still in pain?"

"Yes," wailed Gracie, leaning on Sophie. "My thigh! I can't believe Bandit bit me, right there!

All I was doing was hanging his hay net."

Jess watched as Ava and her mum exchanged a horrified glance, and had to stop herself smiling. *Brilliant, Gracie!* Sophie and Gracie headed off as Lainey returned, her arms full of tack, before Amina jumped in.

"Lainey, help!" Jess heard Amina cry. "Mini is on the chicken-house roof!"

Lainey rolled her eyes, placing the saddle down on the nearest stable door with a sigh, as if Mini climbing on the chicken-house roof was an everyday occurrence.

"I'm so sorry," she apologised to Ava and her mum. "I'd better get her off. She's so heavy, she'll break it."

Willow had sidled over now.

"Mini's a sheep," she said to Ava, who just gaped in astonishment. Then Willow looked over at the tack.

"Oh!" she said in a worried voice. "Lainey forgot his martingale. He chucks his head around, so you'll need one on to stop it. And he'll need a stronger bit too."

Jess crossed her fingers behind her back.

"Definitely – it's the strongest pelham bit he wears, isn't it?" she added. "And I wonder if Lainey remembered to add his calming supplement to his breakfast today?"

To her surprise, Ava blinked, looking uncertainly at her mum.

"What's a martingale? And why would he need a calming supplement?" Ava whispered in a horrified tone.

And suddenly Jess realised: Ava and her mum

must be new to ponies! Jess had assumed they were really experienced, judging by Ava's clothes and the sticker in the car, and the way they had talked about their yard and trainer. But Ava didn't even know what a really basic bit of tack was! They had obviously been lied to. Jess guessed that Rhiannon and her mum knew Ava wouldn't be jumping, or only a low cross-pole at most, and Bandit hadn't bucked until the jumps got bigger. It was a dirty rotten thing to do! She knew Ava couldn't risk riding Bandit. She had to get straight to it, trouble, or no trouble.

"I fell off Bandit this morning – he had a bucking fit," Jess blurted out. "I don't know what you've been told, but it can't have been the truth."

And with that Lainey reappeared, a grinning Amina trotting beside her.

"Sorry!" Amina was saying cheerfully. "She jumped off the roof *literally* as you came round the corner."

"Sorry again," Lainey said to Ava and her mum. "No more distractions. Do you want to follow me?"

But Ava's mum, who was looking more horrified by the second, shook her head, tugging on Ava's arm.

"Actually," she said, "we've changed our minds. I don't think Bandit is the pony for us after all."

And with that, Ava and her mum turned around and headed quickly back towards their car, leaving Lainey looking confused.

"Are you sure?" she called back. Jess wondered if it was her imagination, but Lainey sounded relieved.

"Quite sure!" the woman said firmly, hopping into her seat as an upset-looking Ava climbed in beside her. "That pony sounds awful!"

CHAPTER 7

Jess shuffled her feet. She knew she'd done the right thing, but she hoped Lainey wouldn't be cross. She realised she and her friends, and Lainey, should have just told Ava's mum straight out, but presumed they were really experienced horse people.

"Girls?" Lainey addressed them all but was looking directly at Jess. "What did you say to them?"

Jess looked at her friends, who were all nervously twiddling their hands. It was her doing – she'd told everyone to go ahead – so she needed to take the blame, however bad the consequences would be. She thought about the puppy classes, but she'd done the right thing. She hoped…

"It was me," she said. "I told them about this morning."

Lainey nodded.

"I think you'd better come to my office."

"So you see," Jess explained, after telling Lainey what had happened. "When we realised Ava didn't know what a martingale was, we knew she wasn't experienced! She could have been badly hurt. If he'd been OK, they would have bought him for sure and then Ava would have fallen at home once she'd started jumping."

Lainey looked thoughtful. She didn't seem cross at all. Instead, she really did seem relieved, just like Jess had thought when she heard Lainey talking to Ava's mum.

"OK," Lainey said. "I'm really glad Ava didn't ride him. We don't know if this morning was a one off, or a regular thing, it's what we've seen against what his owners say. Even though he's not mine, I would have felt responsible if they'd bought a pony that wasn't right for her. And yet Rhiannon's mum told me that the girl trying him was experienced. I just don't understand."

"I think she counted on Ava only riding him on the flat, or over a pole at most," Jess said, remembering her earlier thoughts. "And it would have been easy for Ava to fall in love with him, wouldn't it?"

Like I have, she thought sadly.

Lainey nodded.

"Yes," she said. "He is a lovely pony. So why are they so desperate to get rid of him so fast?" She looked troubled. "You're right, Jess. He does have some sort of problem, something that makes them want to wash their hands of him, and quickly!"

"So what do we do?" Jess said, and Lainey smiled.

"What we'll do is hold him here until they return from their holiday. I won't let anyone come and try him out. We can explain that we *think* he has a problem, and then they can sort out whatever issue he might have before they sell him. I'm sorry that I can't do more. As he's not my pony, there's only so much involvement I can have. But we *can* do this for him."

"Thank you," Jess smiled. Feeling a million times better, she headed out to the yard. Lainey wouldn't be taking Bandit on for the riding school as she'd hoped, but at least Jess felt she'd helped him in some small way. She hadn't got into trouble – in fact, quite the opposite. And best of all, she still had the rest of camp to enjoy with him. Even though she couldn't ride Bandit, she would enjoy looking after him. She just loved being around him!

But later, Jess's bubble burst completely. She'd had a brilliant fast hack on Sorrel with her friends. Camp was fun again! She'd just finished making up hay nets and was now combing out Bandit's dark grey mane. With three ponies to help look after, she was super busy, but that was exactly how she liked it. She had absolutely no chance to get into any trouble!

"There you go," she chattered away to Bandit. "You look perfect."

Jess was so engrossed in her task she didn't notice Lainey standing in the doorway. As she glanced up, alerted by Lainey clearing her throat, Jess felt icy prickles on her arms. The look on Lainey's face told her she had bad news, and Jess knew it would involve Bandit!

"Jess," Lainey said, and she sounded serious. "I'm so sorry to tell you, but I've just spoken to Rhiannon's mum in Spain again. I think Ava's mum might have given her a piece of her mind. Rhiannon's mum was *really* unhappy about the fact I won't let anyone ride Bandit and is adamant that he's never behaved like that before, and she wouldn't hear of him staying here until they got back…" Lainey looked sad. "She's arranged for a horse dealer to pick Bandit up tomorrow afternoon, who will then sell him on. By the sounds of it, they just want him gone quickly, and it doesn't matter who to!"

"And Lainey can't do any more?" Willow said glumly. She was sitting on a hay-bale with the rest of Jess's friends. They'd all gathered around Jess in the cool of the barn, where the sweet meadow

hay filled the air with the scent of summer. Jess had just told her friends what Lainey had told her, and as she shook her head, tears started to fall, hot and splashy.

She couldn't bear the thought of Bandit being taken away. Jess had read horror stories of ponies with problems being given medicines to disguise pain, and then being sold on again and again, eventually ending up in markets where the only person who'd want them was... Actually, she didn't want to think about that. It was too horrible!

"No," she sniffed, in answer to Willow's question. "The stables don't have the money to go investigating what is wrong with someone else's pony," she explained, relaying what Lainey had told her. "And although Lainey *is* looking for another pony, she's not going to take one on with any sort of possible health issue."

"It's such a shame that we can't find out what's

wrong with Bandit," Poppy said. "Just in case it's something really simple. I wish he could tell us."

As everyone agreed that this was indeed a shame, Jess's mind started to race. What if there *was* some way to find out what was wrong with Bandit? She didn't know if it would stop him being taken away, but it might help him, somehow? And she knew exactly who to ask. She remembered her promise to her mum and dad, but she knew she had to sneak out to Asia's surgery somehow. She had to try – for Bandit. His future was at stake and right now that was all that mattered!

CHAPTER 8

It was easy in the end, slipping away. Jess waited until supper was over, after which the camp members had some free time. Asia's veterinary clinic was only a mile away. Jess walked further to school, and she knew the town well. She'd thought about ringing Asia on the phone her mum had left for emergencies but Asia wasn't the best at picking up, especially if she was busy. And if Jess left an answerphone message, it might be too late! She had to see her, in person.

With the others keeping guard, Jess crept out of the gates, down the leafy lane and on to the pavement towards the high street. One of the reasons Sunshine Stables were so popular was that Vale Farm was right on the edge of town, making it easy for children to get to their riding lessons without having to rely on lifts.

Crossing over the main road, Jess marched on. It was a huge risk, sneaking out. If Lainey found out, she could be sent home! That would definitely blow her chances with her mum and dad. But there was her cousin's surgery ahead, a modern building on one of the street corners. Jess gave a sigh of relief as she saw the lights were on. She'd done it now.

Although the surgery was closed, Asia often stayed on later to write up her notes and prepare for the next day's visits. Jess knocked on the back door and hopped from foot to foot as her big cousin opened it, a look of surprise on her face.

"Jessy!" Asia gave her a hug. "What are you doing here? I thought you were at camp." She looked worried. "Jess, are you in trouble?"

"Yes, I'm meant to be at camp, and, no, I'm not in trouble," Jess explained, crossing her fingers. She *really* hoped she wasn't anyway! "But I need to talk to you. There's a pony who needs my help, and I don't know what to do!"

Placing an arm around her shoulders, Asia ushered Jess into the surgery, where a variety of animals dozed or sniffed a hello to her.

"Now," said Asia, "What's going on?"

Jess took a deep breath.

"There's a pony at the stables," she began. "Bandit. Not one of Lainey's, he's there waiting to be sold. He's come from this super-posh yard where he has to stay in his stable all the time because he does all these big shows. But for some reason, the girl who owned him wasn't riding him anymore. Lainey thought he would be brilliant for the riding school, but then I rode him…" And Jess told Asia how Bandit had been practically perfect but had exploded when Jess tried him over the bigger jumps. "He just went crazy," Jess explained. "It was so out of character."

Asia nodded, looking serious.

"Did you have to nudge him on, to jump him bigger?" she asked.

"Yes," Jess said, remembering that Lainey had told her to ride forward. "I did."

"OK," Asia said thoughtfully. "And can you think of anything else that has happened since he arrived? What was he like in the stable?"

"So sweet and friendly," Jess said. "The only time I saw him put his ears back was when I did

up his girth." She then gave a start, and looked at Asia. "Do you think they're connected?"

"That's what I'm wondering," Asia replied. "And he's going to a horse dealers?"

"Yes," Jess said miserably. This time tomorrow, Bandit would be gone.

"It makes me mad," Asia said crossly. "It definitely sounds like he's uncomfortable. And if the problem's not treated then his behaviour will just get worse and it could be really dangerous."

Then she paused.

"I've got some time off tomorrow morning," she said. "What if I came to see him? I could bring my mobile gastroscope, which would let me look inside his tummy with a tiny camera. I'm not saying I'd find what's wrong, but from what you've described, there's something I'd like to investigate…"

Jess wasn't sure if she'd misheard Asia at first.

"Really?" she stammered, hesitating, a glimmer of hope appearing. But that soon disappeared as she thought about the bill. Asia would need paying and veterinary treatment could be really expensive! She doubted Rhiannon's mum would want to pay and Jess couldn't just go spending Lainey's money. She remembered what Lainey had said, about how taking Bandit in to sell would help pay for the riding-school ponies' winter feed.

"But you can't," she said miserably. "It would cost loads and I don't have any way to pay you."

"Look," Asia said with a smile. "You've worked for us here for so many school holidays. You've never had any pocket money."

Jess thought about this. It hadn't even occurred to her! She did the jobs because she enjoyed doing them. For every cup of tea she made and every floor she mopped, there was the chance to go out in Asia's car to look at ponies, which made it all worthwhile.

"So this can be my way of paying you back," Asia continued. "But," and she looked really serious, "there's only one condition. Will you promise me something?"

Jess nodded. "Anything," she said passionately.

"OK," Asia replied. "Then promise me you'll get your head down at school, and no more detentions." She paused. "I know a little about what's been happening, why you couldn't come for a bit last term, and I know your mum and dad were thinking of stopping you coming over to help with the puppy classes, and I don't blame them. But," and she smiled kindly, "I also know you've been given another chance. You'll be the best vet one day, but you *need* to try to stay out of trouble."

Jess flushed with pride. And although she'd already promised her mum and dad to try harder at school, the fact her promise now meant she could help Bandit meant she was even more determined to keep her word.

"I will," she said, and she meant it. She'd do anything for the beautiful grey pony.

Asia picked up her mobile phone.

"I'm going to call Lainey," she said. "I'll tell her you called me, so you don't get into trouble for sneaking out. That white lie can be on me, but that one only. Although I'm glad you came to see me. I can see how passionate you are about this pony. And I'll walk you back to the yard too." She paused, and smiled at Jess. "I'll do my best for Bandit. If you love him, that's enough for me to at least try!"

CHAPTER 9

Jess could hardly sleep that night. She'd managed to get back into the yard just as free time ended and had gone straight to the ponies to do her chores, her mind racing. To her relief, Lainey had agreed for Asia to take a look at Bandit in the morning, on the basis that his owners *had* said it was OK to get the vet if he needed it, and had signed a special form, giving their consent. Lainey had told Jess she insisted all owners signed the forms before their ponies came onto the yard. Now she knew what she knew, Jess wondered if Rhiannon's mum had been reluctant to.

"Lainey is happy for me to come and see him," Asia had told Jess after she'd finished the call. "And thanks to you," she added, "it won't cost his owners anything. I imagine they'll be pleased."

But Jess remembered that Rhiannon hadn't even said goodbye to Bandit, and the fact they had arranged for the horse dealer to pick him up so quickly. She wasn't so sure. Sighing, she looked up at the horseshoe on the wall. Jess and the other girls had found it on their very first day of camp, and later discovered it had belonged to Fable's mother, Rosie. They'd hung it up to bring them good luck for the week. Jess could only hope the luck would come, and that Bandit would still be at Sunshine Stables camp by the end of tomorrow.

Jess placed her arms around Bandit's smooth grey neck the next morning. She'd mucked out Sorrel and Merlin and then taken her time on Bandit's stable before giving him a groom, carefully combing out his mane and tail, and brushing his coat until it gleamed.

"I'm sorry," she stroked Bandit as he nudged her, eager for his breakfast. "You can't have anything to eat before your examination, you know what Asia said. But I promise you, we're doing this for you, to find out what's wrong."

Then as a familiar car pulled slowly into the yard, and its driver got out to rummage in the back for her equipment, Jess led Bandit out into the sunshine, her hands shaking. What if Asia found something really serious? Something that wasn't fixable? She couldn't bear to think about that.

"Morning." Asia greeted Jess with a hug, and then shook Lainey's hand. "Let's see what's going on, shall we?"

"Oh, Jess he's lovely," Asia said a little while later. She'd just taken his temperature and listened to his heart. Now she had her scoping equipment at the ready, and Bandit had been sedated, ready for his examination.

"Isn't he," Lainey agreed. "I must say, I'm becoming attached to him, despite the bucking. He's such a sweet pony. He seems quite happy here. And he seems to really like Jess too."

Jess felt her heart swell with pride, but it made her more scared too. She had already formed a real bond with Bandit.

Jess could hardly look as Asia passed the gastroscope up Bandit's nostril, even though her cousin had reassured her Bandit wouldn't feel a thing.

"Right then," Asia said. "Let's have a closer look."

Jess didn't really understand what Asia was

studying on the screen as she moved the scope around carefully. But Lainey seemed to know, crouching down so she could take a closer look.

"There," Asia said, and Lainey murmured as if in agreement, never taking her eyes off the screen. "As I suspected. Stomach ulcers. No wonder he didn't want to jump when he was nudged on – he must have been in pain."

Jess felt the blood drain from her face.

"So what does it mean?" she stammered. "Will he need an operation?"

Asia straightened up and gave Bandit a pat.

"No," she said kindly. "He won't. We've got some special medication which will heal his sore stomach, and after that he'd need a change in his care. Ideally I'd like to see him turned out as much as possible so he can graze and relax. It sounds as though his previous home didn't suit him very well. Being stabled all the time, and perhaps being stressed too."

"His owner has a new pony he doesn't get on with," Jess said. "And all he did was go to shows."

Asia nodded.

"That could be it. Sounds like he needs a change of lifestyle." She frowned. "Really, it was

easy to spot, which was lucky. Bandit has stomach ulcers, and it was fairly easy to diagnose. My brain started ticking, Jess, when you mentioned the way he'd put his ears back as you tightened the girth," she paused. "Makes you wonder why his owners didn't try and find out?"

Jess looked at Lainey, who was frowning, and she could tell she was thinking the same thing.

"All done," Asia then said. "I'll just wait a bit, see that he comes out of his sedation OK, and then I've got to get on for my afternoon appointments. I can, of course, get you his medicine, and I'd like to come back in a few weeks, to see how he's doing. If he's still here..."

Her words hung heavily in the air. *If.*

But after Asia had had a cup of coffee, checked Bandit over and given Jess a hug before driving out of the yard, Lainey turned to Jess.

"I'm glad we found out what's wrong," she

said heavily. "But I'm afraid I still can't take him on. You see, I don't know if he'll be suitable – even when he's better. I know nothing about his history, only what Emily has told me." She looked really sad, Jess thought. "I can't take the risk. I'm going to speak to Rhiannon's mum and explain what we've found and get her to cancel the horse dealer," Lainey continued. "I'll happily keep him here until he recovers, save him the stress of being moved again. At least then we know he won't be sold on with a problem. If I lose money, I lose money – so be it..." She shrugged, and then frowned as her mobile bleeped. Pulling it out of her pocket, she peered at the screen. Jess held her breath as Lainey's frown deepened.

"The horse dealer is running ahead of schedule," Lainey said in alarm. "He'll be here in an hour! But I haven't been able to get hold of anyone yet!"

JESS and the JUMPY PONY

One hour. One precious hour left with the pony Jess already believed was her horsey soulmate. His sedation had worn off now, and he was back to his sweet self, snuggling into Jess's elbow. The minutes were ticking by, far too fast. She'd cried so many tears into his mane and her face was blotchy and red. Amina and Willow had come to comfort her, but she just wanted to be alone with Bandit.

Lainey had been calling Rhiannon's mum constantly, each time getting visibly more stressed, but she hadn't picked up. *Probably sunbathing or swimming*, Jess thought bitterly, wiping her eyes. They didn't care about Bandit. All Lainey could do was pass over the notes Asia had hastily written up, but there was no guarantee anything would be done for the sweet grey pony.

Unless she, Jess, did something…

She wiped her eyes and thought about what the

old Jess would have done. The hot-headed Jess who got detentions at school. The Jess she'd promised her mum and dad she wouldn't be. And suddenly, she had an idea. If they could just buy some time, it would give Lainey a chance to talk to Rhiannon's mum. Jess had promised everyone she'd stay out of trouble, but this was a pony emergency!

Before she could talk herself out of it, she slipped Bandit's head collar on and quietly led him outside, scanning the yard. Zoe was helping some of the girls clean bridles in the tack room and Lainey was up in the top fields.

Looking left and right, Jess urged Bandit on towards the hay barn. Peeking around the corner to check the coast was clear, she led Bandit inside, past the bales and down the old corridor which led to the unused stables, now full of rickety jumps and pallets and boxes.

There was just enough room to lead Bandit

into the very end stable, all spidery and dusty and dark. Perching on an old wooden barrel, Jess then held Bandit still, stroking his ears gently. She'd managed to quickly stuff her pockets with pony nuts, and she fed them to him one at a time as she looked anxiously at her watch.

The dealer would be here any minute, and she was counting on him to be the sort of man who wouldn't have time to wait around for a missing pony. *Or maybe he will,* she thought, her stomach lurching as she heard the chug of a lorry. But it was too late now. She had hidden Bandit as best she could in the few minutes she'd had, and she just had to hope no one found them, until the lorry had left...

CHAPTER 10

Jess was sure the whole yard would hear her heart thumping through her camp T-shirt as she held as still as possible. The minutes were ticking by … five … ten … fifteen … her arms and legs ached, but she didn't dare move, just in case Bandit moved too. He was being so quiet, gently snuffling into Jess's hand for the pony nuts, which were fast running out.

Holding her breath, she tried to work out what was going on outside. She could hear a man's angry raised voice, heavy footsteps clomping back and forth, and a door banging. Still no reassuring sound of a lorry engine starting up, which would mean Bandit was safe. Then to her horror, she heard the squeak of the barn door, soft footsteps on the carpet of hay, the clatter of a jump wing being moved over, where Jess had hurriedly tried to block the path to the very furthest stable.

Her stomach was doing a loop the loop, and her breathing was fast and ragged, tears spilling over. She'd been found, and Bandit would be gone. She knew she'd blown everything. No puppy classes with Asia, no more helping her out at the surgery. But Jess knew deep down she wouldn't have done anything differently. Squeezing her eyes shut as the last door was opened and a chink of light fell on to Bandit's soft grey coat, she wrapped her arms around him one final time.

"I'm sorry, boy," she whispered, choking back a sob. "I tried my best."

She expected to hear the gruff tones of the horse

dealer, or the upset ones of Lainey. But instead, a gentle voice broke through her thoughts.

"Jess?"

Emily? Jess peered round Bandit's neck, as Lainey's daughter reached forwards and gave Bandit a pat.

"Jess?" Emily repeated, and Jess shuffled out, wiping her teary face with her hands, leaving streaks in the dust. "It's OK," Emily said, a rare smile appearing on her face. "Bandit's staying here, at Sunshine Stables."

"I … I still don't understand," Jess said a short while later. She was perched on the stone mounting block, clutching Bandit's lead rope. Her friends were gathered round her and Lainey was standing next to Bandit, a big smile on her face. Emily was sitting next to Jess, with her brother Jack on the lower step of the block, as they all listened intently.

"I thought he was going to be sold?" Jess continued, still trying to make sense of it all. "I thought he was leaving. The lorry was here and everything."

"Well," Lainey said. "He was, and it was, and the horse dealer wasn't very happy, but hey ho.

JESS *and the* JUMPY PONY

It was all very last minute. Emily, why don't you explain?"

Emily looked up, her expression a little shy.

"I thought Bandit was a really good pony," she said. "When Rhiannon stopped taking him to shows, I couldn't understand why. She said he wasn't able to jump big enough so she'd got a new pony. But when I found out about his poor tummy, I…" She paused, looking upset. "I couldn't believe that Rhiannon's parents hadn't tried to work out what was wrong. I sort of knew Bandit's old owner from pony club, so I sent her a message from Mum's phone and she rang Mum straight away, and sent loads of photos over." She looked at Lainey, who smiled.

"It turned out Bandit *was* a dream pony," Lainey explained, taking up the story. "He's a good jumper, although it *is* true he wasn't able to jump as high as Rhiannon wanted, so she quickly lost interest, and that would explain why they weren't so bothered about sorting out his problems. But his old owner told me he's a brilliant schoolmaster. Not only did all the children in his old family learn to ride on him, but he was also loaned out to Meadow Hall riding school in Buckley," she said, and Jess recognised the name of a town a few miles away. "So I rang them, and they gave glowing references. They loved him! We had to be really quick, and when Rhiannon's mum finally rang me back from Spain, just as the horse dealer arrived, I bought him, over the phone. It couldn't have been more last minute, really."

Jess was silent for a few seconds as she took it all in. Then she grinned, jumping up and hugging Lainey, and even Emily, and most of all Bandit, over and over.

"So Bandit's here to stay?" she said to Lainey. "For good?"

JESS and the JUMPY PONY

"For good," Lainey smiled. "Remember, he'll need some time to come right first, for his stomach ulcers to heal, but we think he'll be worth it, and hopefully by next summer he'll be a brilliant camp pony. I can't wait to see him out grazing in the fields with all his new pony friends. I told you I'd grown attached!" She patted the sweet grey pony, her eyes warm. "Welcome to your new home, Bandit! And, Jess, it's all thanks to you."

A short while later, just before her lesson on Sorrel, Jess couldn't resist sneaking five minutes with Bandit in his stable. It still didn't feel real, in the best possible way. Lainey had spoken with Jess and told her she would love her help over the coming weeks and months with Bandit, to help him through his recovery. Lainey had also rung her mum and to Jess's huge relief, she wasn't angry at all. Quite the opposite actually.

"She was really proud of you," Lainey had told Jess. "For using your initiative, and for trusting your instincts, and she said she'll let your dad know. Well done. Your mum told me you'll make a great vet one day, and I agree."

Jess hadn't hesitated in saying yes to helping out with Bandit's care. It had given her a new sense of purpose. With the beautiful grey pony to look after and the puppy classes at Asia's surgery, plus her commitment to try really hard at school, she felt completely content! Jess smiled as Bandit left his hay and came over to say hello. She was learning all his ways, like his sweet habit of burying his muzzle in the crook of her arm.

Hearing footsteps, she glanced up to see Emily walking over.

Jess smiled. "Hey," she said, and Emily gave a small smile back.

"Hey," she muttered in return, but she stopped

to pat Bandit. For a few seconds there was an awkward silence.

"Thank you," Jess said finally. "For everything you did, finding out about Bandit's past."

"It's fine," Emily replied. "When I found out about Rhiannon getting rid of him, sending him to the horse dealer I… We've been friends since reception, but recently…" She shook her head, looking upset. "Let's just say she wasn't the person I thought she was. I always looked up to her – she's this amazing rider and she's really popular – but looking back, I'm not sure she was ever such a great friend. She could be quite mean actually. And she's not a true horse lover. Not like you."

Jess thought about Rhiannon and the way she'd talked to Emily the day Bandit had been dropped off. It must have hurt Emily to see the way her friend treated her pony, especially in comparison to the way Emily doted on Fable. Bandit hadn't

been good enough for Rhiannon, and when there
had been a problem, instead of finding out what
was wrong, she had wanted to get rid of him as
quickly as possible.

"Thank you," Jess said. "And so are you. A true
horse lover."

Emily smiled.

"Yeah," she said. "I am. The best way to be."
Then she paused. "Really, it was all down to
you," she said. "Mum told me it was because you
believed in Bandit in the first place. She said it
was a really brave thing to do – standing up for
Bandit like you did and hiding him. She said not
many people would have done that."

Jess felt a warm glow inside her and the two
girls were silent for a minute as Bandit snuffled
between them.

Then Emily straightened up and the spell was
broken.

JESS and the JUMPY PONY

"Actually," she began in her usual bossy voice. "I came over to ask something. Can you sort out Sorrel's saddle pad? I noticed it still had loads of hair on it. You need to…" She paused, and seemed to change her mind. "Oh, it doesn't matter." And she wandered off, leaving Jess chuckling. That was more like the Emily she knew, although perhaps now Emily realised the camp members loved horses as much as she did! She gave Bandit one final hug, running her hands gently over his soft ears.

"You'll have an amazing life here, out in the fields," she told him quietly. "I'll see you as much as possible, and when you're better, you'll love all the lessons and hacks and cross-country jumping."

She thought about what Emily had just said. "I believed in you from the start," she whispered. Bandit gave a sigh as Jess placed her forehead against his, breathing in his lovely warm pony smell: citronella spray mixed with the comforting biscuity scent of horsehair.

"We were meant to find each other. You'll take care of me and I'll take care of you," she continued. "Thank you for choosing me to tell your story to."

ACKNOWLEDGEMENTS

Thank you to Julian Radburn, our wonderful Equine Vet at Damory Veterinary Clinic, who advised me on Bandit's problems, treatment, and recovery.

ARE YOU A PERFECT PONY PRO? TAKE THIS QUIZ TO FIND OUT!

1   WHICH OF THESE IS A "STABLE VICE"?

a) Weaving

b) Looming

c) Plaiting

2   CHESTNUT FOALS CAN TURN GREY IN COLOUR AS THEY GET OLDER. TRUE OR FALSE?

a) True

b) False

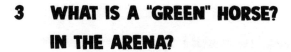

**3 WHAT IS A "GREEN" HORSE?
IN THE ARENA?**

a) A horse which lives out all year round

b) A young horse in the early stages of ridden training

c) A poorly horse

4 HOW CAN YOU ROUGHLY DETERMINE A HORSE'S AGE?

a) By the number of grey hairs around their muzzle

b) By their teeth

c) The length of their mane

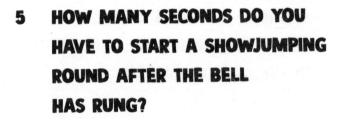

5 HOW MANY SECONDS DO YOU HAVE TO START A SHOWJUMPING ROUND AFTER THE BELL HAS RUNG?

a) Ten

b) Two hundred

c) Forty-five

6 WHEN WARMING UP IN A COMPETITION ARENA HOW SHOULD YOU PASS OTHERS?

a) Left shoulder to left shoulder

b) As quickly as possible on either side

c) Halt and wait for them to ride around you

7 WHAT IS THE SENSITIVE TRIANGLE LOCATED ON THE UNDERSIDE OF A HORSE'S HOOF CALLED?

a) A toad

b) A newt

c) A frog

8 HOW MANY FAULTS ARE GIVEN FOR A POLE KNOCK DOWN IN A SHOWJUMPING ROUND?

a) Ten

b) One

c) Four

ANSWERS TO THE QUIZ!

Answers: 1a, 2a, 3b, 4b, 5c, 6a, 7c, 8c